# GET READY FOR GABí!

## PLEASE DON'T GO!

by Marisa Montes

illustrated by Joe Cepeda

> \* That's Gabí. As in Ga-BEE. With an
> accent. Not Gabi. 'Cause that's the way
> she likes it. Oh, and it does NOT rhyme with
> blabby! And she does NOT talk too much!

A
**LITTLE APPLE**
PAPERBACK

SCHOLASTIC INC.
New York  Toronto  London  Auckland  Sydney
Mexico City  New Delhi  Hong Kong  Buenos Aires

ISBN 0-439-47523-6
Text copyright © 2004 by Marisa Montes
Illustrations copyright © 2004 by Scholastic Inc.
SCHOLASTIC, LITTLE APPLE, and associated logos are trademarks
and/or registered trademarks of Scholastic Inc.

12 11 10 9 8 7 6 5 4 3 2                    4 5 6 7 8 9/0

Printed in the U.S.A.                              40
First printing, June 2004

# CONTENTS

*In memory of*
*Mamota, mi abuelita,*
*Juanita Cardona Montes*
*June 14, 1901–May 9, 1986*

# Acknowledgments

Special thanks to the staff of the Lindsay Wildlife Museum of Walnut Creek, California, for all their help and input in my research of injured wild animals and of home rehabilitation programs. In particular, I'd like to thank Marie Travers, Wildlife Rehabilitation Manager, for all the time she spent instructing me on "opos" and on the At-Home Care Program. The fictional John Muir Wildlife Museum is loosely drawn from the Lindsay Wildlife Museum.

Thanks also to my friends, Susan Middleton Elya and Raquel Victoria Rodríguez, for all your feedback and encouragement, and especially to Corinne Hawkins for the brainstorming sessions and for cluing me in about the Wildlife At-Home Care Program. And thanks to Katherine Flores, Upper Grade Title 1 Reading specialist at Cambridge Elementary School in Concord, California, for checking the kid-friendliness of this story.

Finally, thanks to my aunt, Dr. Carmín Montes Cumming, for always being my Spanish consultant and for being a great fan and admirer of Gabí. And a Gabí-the-Great thank-you to Maria S. Barbo for her excellent editor's eye in helping me to weave together all the elements of this story.

— M. M.

## UNO
## CHAPTER 1
# "STAY WITH US FOREVER!"

*"Había una vez, y dos son tres . . ."*

Abuelita always starts her stories that way. It means, "There was one time, and two makes three . . ." It sounds kind of goofy in English, but it works in Spanish. And Abuelita only speaks Spanish.

Abuelita is my grandmother. She's been visiting us from Puerto Rico for the past few months and hasn't learned English yet.

That's okay, though, because my family *always* speaks Spanish at home. Mami and Papi say, that way, we'll never forget how to speak it. And with school and watching TV,

1

my four-year-old brother, Miguelito, and I have learned English really well, too. We practice English at school and hear it when we watch TV.

Anyway, Miguelito and I were planning to teach Abuelita some English soon.

All three of us were snuggled in Abuelita's bed: She was in the middle, and Miguelito and I cuddled up on either side of her, like a cream-filled *galleta*. That's a cookie — *yum*!

Mami and Papi had gone to some fancy party at Mami's work. Whenever the three of us

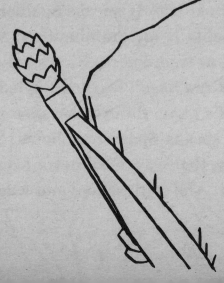

are alone at night, Miguelito and I sneak into Abuelita's room. Then we climb into bed with her, and she tells us stories from Puerto Rico.

When we first crawled into her bed tonight, Miguelito had yelled, "Tell us a story about *el cuco*!"

I groaned. "*Recuerda, Miguelito.* Remember, every time you hear stories about the bogeyman at night, you get *pesadillas.*"

"*Es verdad.*" Abuelita nodded. "It is true. You do get nightmares. How about Juan Bobo instead?"

Abuelita knows lots of Juan Bobo stories. He's a silly boy from Puerto Rico who always gets things mixed-up or backward.

"*YAY!*" we yelled, bouncing on the bed.

She started telling us our favorite Juan Bobo story: It's the one about the time Juan Bobo decided to take the family pig to church. He dressed the pig in his mother's best Sunday dress. Then he put all his mother's jewelry on the pig's ears and neck and fat toes. And he put makeup and lipstick on the pig's face.

On the way to church, the pig saw a mud hole and bolted for it. When his mother saw what Juan Bobo had done to her things, he couldn't sit down for a week!

Even though Miguelito and I had heard the story lots of times, we snuggled close and listened to every word. When Abuelita got to the part about the pig jumping into the mud hole all dressed up in Juan Bobo's mother's best things, we laughed and laughed till our tummies hurt.

Abuelita tells the best stories ever!

"*Y colorín, colorado, este cuento se ha acabado*," she said. That's the way she always ends her stories. It's a long, silly way to say "the end."

"You're the best storyteller in the whole wide world!" Miguelito said. "I could listen to you tell that story a trillion jillion times. Tell it again! *¡Otra vez!¡Otra vez!¡Otra vez!*"

He must be a mind reader because I was thinking the same thing.

I sat up on my knees and hugged Abuelita as hard as I could. "Me, too!"

"*OOOF!*" Abuelita laughed. "*¡Qué abrazote!*"

I sat back on my heels and took her hand. "Abuelita, promise me something," I said, squeezing her hand. "Promise that you won't go back to Puerto Rico, and you'll live with us forever! Promise."

"*Sí, Abuelita, ¡promételo!*" Miguelito began to hop from knee to knee. "Promise! Promise!Promise!"

Abuelita glanced at the picture of my grandpa on her nightstand.

She gave us a sad smile and patted my hand. "Don't you think you'll get tired of your old *abuelita*?"

"Never!" we cried, jumping on the bed. "Promise! Promise! Please! *Pleeeeease!*"

"*¡Shhh, niños! Calladitos, por favor.*" Abuelita laughed. "We'll see."

The smile faded from my face, and I stopped jumping.

Miguelito hugged her. He's too young to know better.

But I'm not. "We'll see" is what grown-ups say when they really mean "No, but I don't want to argue about it."

Now all the weird things Abuelita had been doing in the past month made sense.

Last week, I heard Abuelita tell Mami

that she misses visiting Abuelito at the cemetery. (He's buried in Ciales, their hometown.) The week before that, she showed Miguelito and me pictures of the pretty beaches in Puerto Rico and told  us how warm the ocean is there. And lately, she'd filled her room with more and more pictures of my cousins from Puerto Rico.

Then, the other day, I heard her talking all hush-hush to Tío Julio on the phone. He's the one who brought her here for a surprise visit. What if . . . ?

*No! Abuelita can't leave us! Abuelita is fun, and much better than any old babysitter could ever be! And if she goes back to Puerto Rico, we'll only see her once a year.*

There *had* to be something I could do to make her stay. After all, I'm Maritza Gabriela Morales Mercado, otherwise known as Gabí the Great!

I was sure I could think of *something*!

But what?

## DOS
## CHAPTER 2
## "YIKES!"

"Devin! Jasmine!" I called out as I ran up to them at our usual meeting place the next morning.

Devin Suzuki and Jasmine Lange are my best friends. We always walk to school together.

Jasmine spun around. Her black curls bounced. "What's up?"

"I need your help, you guys," I said, all out of breath from running. "I think Abuelita is planning to move back to Puerto Rico. I have to figure out a way to make her stay."

"Oh, no!" Devin said. "I *love* your

*abuelita*. And I'll miss practicing my Spanish with her."

Devin's family lived in Panama for a few years because of her dad's job. That was before they moved here to Northern California. Devin learned to speak Spanish really well, and she doesn't want to forget it.

Jasmine groaned. "I'll miss the yummy after-school snacks she makes."

I stared at them. "What you're *missing* is the point! You're acting like she's already gone. She is *not* leaving. I've decided."

I stomped a spunky foot to show them I meant business. "I just have to figure out *how* to make her stay. So you guys have to put on your thinking caps and help me."

The corners of Devin's lips turned down. "How can we — ?"

But that's when we walked into our classroom. We were almost late and our teacher, Mr. Fine, was already writing the date on the board.

Real quick, we slipped into our desks. We're super lucky that Mr. F lets us sit next to one another.

"All right, class." Mr. F clapped his hands. "Settle down."

We sat up straight.

"Today, we'll start a new project," said Mr. Fine. "It's called 'Discovering Ourselves.' We have such a culturally diverse classroom, it would be nice to learn about one another's ethnic backgrounds."

Jasmine raised her hand. "What does *culturally diverse* mean, Mr. Fine?"

"Good question, Jasmine." Mr. F nodded. "It means most of you or your parents or their parents come from different countries."

Johnny Wiley, the class bully, turned to me and snickered. "Yeah, and some come from different planets."

Before I could make a face at Johnny, Mr. F leaned down to him.

"That's enough, John," Mr. Fine warned.

He turned back to us. "For this project, you'll work in pairs and teach your partner something about your culture. Then your partner will share what he or she has learned with the class."

I looked at Devin and Jasmine. Which one would I choose to be my partner? And which one would be left on her own?

Then I had an awful thought: *What if they chose to pair up with each other? I'd be the odd girl out!*

Before we could choose, Mr. Fine grabbed his notebook. "I'm going to call out a name and the name of that student's partner."

My jaw dropped open.

Jasmine crossed her eyes. She usually does that when she likes something. But I *knew* that wasn't why she was crossing them this time.

Devin wrinkled her nose. Her lip curled

up so high I could see the braces on her two front teeth. She *hates* for her braces to show.

*Don't we even get to choose our own partner?* I thought.

The rest of the class groaned.

"That's enough, class," Mr. F said. "You'll like this, you'll see." His bushy eyebrows wiggled above his glasses. He was acting like we were going to have oodles of fun — *gozar un montón,* as Mami would say.

I slipped down in my seat. The last time Mr. F chose partners for us, it wasn't *any* fun at *all*!

"Devin Suzuki and Sissy Huffer," Mr. F called out.

Sissy shook her prissy yellow curls and gave Devin a sickly sweet smile.

Devin looked like she'd just swallowed a worm. Sissy is stuck-up — *presumida*. She's always bragging about how great she thinks she is.

Mr. Fine continued. "Jasmine Lange and Billy Wong."

Billy made a chimp face, and Jazz rolled her eyes. They can't stand each other. Billy Wong is Johnny Wiley's best friend.

Mr. F cleared his throat. "Gabí Morales and Johnny Wiley."

I stared at Mr. Fine. He always says my name Ga-BEE 'cause he knows that's what I like. It usually makes me feel special. Not today. Instead, I got tummy-tingles like I had just whooshed down the tallest hill of a roller coaster.

*Me and Johnny Wiley?* Johnny Wiley is absolutely, positively my very WORST *enemigo*!

In fact, he's every girl's worst enemy *and* nightmare! He likes to tease me and my friends and call us names. He even makes fun of my Spanish.

Devin, Jasmine, and I looked at one another. At the same time, we each mouthed, *"¡Caracoles!"*

That means "YIKES!"

I glanced at Johnny. He gave me his nastiest, most Wiley smile.

This was just too much! First, I was losing Abuelita. And now I was being paired up with Wiley the Smiley.

*UGH! I can't be Johnny Wiley's partner!*

I thought. *I'd rather be paired up with a python!*

I couldn't stand it. I jumped up. "No!"

Mr. Fine's head jerked up so fast his glasses flew off his nose. He grabbed them before they landed on the floor.

"Gabí?" he said. "Is there a problem?"

"I . . . I can't do it. I can't work with" — I pointed at Johnny — "*him.*"

Mr. Fine put his glasses back on his nose and peered down at me.

"The purpose of this project, Gabí," said Mr. F, "is to help you learn about the culture of your fellow students. This will help you understand them better. That's why I teamed you up with Johnny. So you two can learn to get along."

Once Mr. F had made up his mind, I knew he wouldn't change it. But I had to try again.

"Please, Mr. Fine?" I begged. "*Pleeease* team me up with someone else!"

Mr. Fine stared at me for a moment.

Then he nodded. "Gabí, I've made my decision. You *will* work with Johnny. But I'll send a note home to your parents. Maybe they can help you understand why it's important to learn to get along with others. Bring the note back tomorrow — *signed* by your parents."

Then Mr. Fine turned to the rest of the class. "And as part of this project, next week, we'll have a special surprise."

I sank to my chair. I didn't even care about Mr. F's special surprise.

*Now Mami and Papi are going to find out that I'm in trouble again,* I thought. *And I'll* still *have to work with Johnny.*

*Fine!* I crossed my arms in front of my chest. *I'll teach Johnny Wiley something about my culture, all right.*

*I'll teach him something in Spanish he'll never forget!*

*That'll be* my *special surprise!*

## TRES
## CHAPTER 3
## LEARNING LANGUAGES

"*¡Hola, Abuelita!*" I yelled as Devin and I ran into my house after school. Mami and Papi were still at work.

"My friends are going to help me teach you English," I told Abuelita. "We're setting up the classroom in the backyard."

This was Phase One of my Keeping Abuelita Plan. (That's my plan to stop her from moving back to Puerto Rico.) But I wouldn't tell her that part.

Thinking of teaching Johnny something in Spanish had given me the idea to start teaching Abuelita English right away. If she learned some English, she might feel happier living here in California. That would make it easier for Miguelito and me to convince her to stay with us forever.

"*¡Qué divino!*" Abuelita clapped. "How delightful!" Then she looked around. "*¿Dónde está Jasmine?*"

"Jasmine went to pick up Lizzie, so she can help, too," I replied.

Lizzie was our newest friend. Her family had recently moved into a house down the block from my family. She doesn't go to our school, but she's lots of fun.

"I'm going to get my boots," I told them. "Abuelita, can you please take the stacking chairs outside? Devin, would you get the chalkboard? I'll tell Miguelito all about it, so he can help, too."

After I told Miguelito, I ran to my room to slip on my red cowgirl boots. My boots help me think better. To teach, I needed to *think*.

Then Devin and I ran to the backyard and started setting up.

A few minutes later, Jasmine slipped through the side gate with Lizzie. Lizzie brought her big golden retriever puppy, Pogo. Pogo was on his leash and stood quietly next to Lizzie. He's really smart and knows how to heel.

"Hope you don't mind," Lizzie said. "Pogo started whimpering when I tried to leave him alone. I usually play with him after school. So I brought him along."

"Sure." I was helping Devin carry the chalkboard. "He can help teach English to Abuelita."

"Hey!" Jazz snapped her fingers. "I've got an even better idea. While you teach your grandmother English, you could teach Lizzie and me some Spanish."

"Yeah." Lizzie nodded. "You could teach Pogo, too, 'cause he doesn't know Spanish yet."

*"Hmm . . ."* I looked up at the sky, thinking. "That could work! I was going to teach Abuelita and Tippy at the same time. Tippy doesn't speak English, either. He just knows Spanish."

Jasmine giggled and crossed her eyes. Tippy is my cat.

I ignored her. "And I know just *how* to do it."

I was extra glad I'd worn my boots. If I was going to teach two languages at the same time, I *really* needed to think.

Just then, Abuelita came out of our house carrying the stackable plastic chairs. She was almost more excited to have me teach her English than I was.

*"¡Hola, muchachas!"* she said.

*"¡Hola, Señora Mercado!"* Lizzie and Jasmine called out.

*"Woof!"* Pogo said hello, too.

*"¡Hola, Devin!"* Miguelito stepped out of

the house, carrying Tippy. But when he spotted Lizzie and Jasmine, he got all shy and hid his face in Tippy's fur.

Miguelito likes my friends. But he gets really shy when there are lots of kids my age around. He thinks we're teenagers, even though we're only in third grade.

Then Miguelito peered out from behind Tippy's fur with one eye.

He spotted Pogo. "Hi, Pogo!"

But Tippy spotted Pogo, too. He started to squirm in Miguelito's arms.

Pogo bolted forward, but Lizzie held his leash tight. "Pogo, sit!"

Pogo sat. *¡Caracoles!* Tippy would *never* sit just because I told him to.

I grabbed Tippy from Miguelito before Tippy could leap away.

Abuelita sat at one end of the row of chairs. I handed Tippy to her.

"*Toma, Abuelita,* would you hold him, *¿por favor?*" I said in Spanish. "You should sit together because you'll both be learning English."

Lizzie sat at the other end of the row. Pogo sat at her feet. We wanted to keep the pets as far apart as possible.

Jasmine and Miguelito sat in the middle chairs. Devin and Miguelito would take turns being my assistant.

Devin placed the chalkboard in front of the chairs, so everyone could see — right next to Abuelita's tree. (We call it Abuelita's tree 'cause she loves to climb it and sit in the branches.)

"Okay, everybody," I said. "I'm going to

teach you a song from Puerto Rico that's in both Spanish and English. That way, everybody can learn a new language at the same time. I made up my own rap tune for it, so everybody can clap and stomp to the beat."

Miguelito translated for Abuelita. She nodded and tried to keep Tippy from squirming on her lap.

"*Quédate quieto, Tippy.*" I told him to keep still. "How are you going to learn if you keep wiggling?"

I turned to Devin. "Devin, will you please draw the words while I teach them to everyone?"

Devin held up some chalk. "I'll use colored chalk."

I nodded and turned to my class. "Okay, repeat after me. *Repite conmigo,*" I told Abuelita.

I started clapping and stomping. "*Pollito*, chicken . . ." I rapped.

Everyone
repeated, and
clapped and stomped.
Well, everyone but Tippy and Pogo. They
were just listening, but at least they weren't
chasing each other.

I nodded and grinned real big. I went on:
*Clap! Stomp! Clap! Stomp!*

"... *Gallina,* hen.
*Lápiz,* pencil, *y*
　　*Pluma,* pen!"

I paused to give everybody a chance to repeat after me. Then I turned to check on
Devin. She had drawn a little chick, a fat hen,
a long skinny pencil, and a short stubby pen.

I nodded and went on to the next verse.
*Clap! Stomp! Clap! Stomp!*

> "*Ventana*, window.
> *Puerta*, door.
> *Maestra*, teacher, *y*
> *Piso*, floor!"

Just as everyone finished the last verse,
a bushy brown squirrel scam-
pered down the trunk of

Abuelita's tree. It stopped right above the chalkboard. When the squirrel saw us, it froze.

Then — *you won't believe this!* — Tippy leaped from Abuelita's lap and pounced on the chalkboard.

The squirrel darted across the lawn with Tippy close behind.

The next moment, Pogo yanked on his leash. Lizzie tugged back, but Pogo ripped the leash from her hand and tore across the yard.

Pogo raced after Tippy and the squirrel.

"Stop!Stop!Stop!" Jasmine and I screamed.

"*¡Para!¡Para!¡Para!*" Devin and Miguelito yelled.

Abuelita and Lizzie ran after Tippy and Pogo, screaming.

"*¡Caracoles!*" I stomped my boot. "Stop, I said! STOP!"

The more we screamed and yelled, the faster the squirrel, Tippy, and Pogo ran in circles around my backyard classroom. And the faster the animals ran, the faster Abuelita and Lizzie ran.

I didn't know Abuelita was such a good runner!

Soon Miguelito, Devin, and Jasmine joined the chase.

But I couldn't move. I just stood there and stared as everyone ran around and around and around me. *At this rate, I'll* never *teach Abuelita English!* I thought.

*That* was the end of my outdoor language class.

And *that* was the end of Phase One of my Keeping Abuelita Plan!

*¡Caracoles!* What would I do *now*?

## CUATRO
## CHAPTER 4
## *SECRETOS* AND TEARS

"Gabí, I have to tell you *un secreto,*" Miguelito whispered in my ear. We'd just finished dinner after my language class, and we were still cleaning up.

Miguelito always has secrets to tell. Sometimes they're just silly. But sometimes, he finds out some good stuff. And he always tells me.

As I led him to the family room, Miguelito kept his lips sucked in tight. He looked like Tippy when he has a cricket in his mouth that he doesn't want to let escape.

"*¿Qué?*" I said.

The moment I asked, "What?" Miguelito screamed: "MAMI AND PA—"

I covered his mouth with my hand. "*Shhh! Cuchichea.* Whisper."

I glanced around, but the adults hadn't noticed.

"Before dinner," he whispered, "Mami and Papi were talking about buying an airplane ticket to Puerto Rico."

Miguelito's big eyes got all watery. "I think it's for Abuelita. Gabí, I don't want her to go!" *Lágrimas* ran down his cheeks.

*So I was right!* I thought. I wiped the tears and hugged my little brother.

Then I turned to look at Abuelita. She and Mami were still in the kitchen, laughing and talking.

My eyes started to fill with tears, too.

"I know, Kikito." I called Miguelito by his pet name. "I don't want her to go, either."

Just then, Papi walked in. He had Mr. Fine's note in one hand and my backpack in the other.

Miguelito spotted Tippy and chased him down the hall. That left Papi and me alone.

"Here, Gabita, take Mr. Fine's note back to school," Papi said, slipping the note in my backpack. I had given the note to him and Mami before dinner. "Your *mami* and I have signed it."

I nodded and sank down on the couch. I stared at my cowgirl boots.

Papi kissed me on the head. "Don't worry, Gabita. *No te apures.* You will learn to get along with Johnny Wiley, and everything will be just fine."

He set down my pack and kicked back in his recliner with the newspaper.

After they had read the note, Mami and Papi had a long talk with me. They both agreed with Mr. Fine: I have to learn to work with everyone, even kids I don't like.

Mami reminded me that even my favorite superhero, Dragon-Ella, has to make friends with bad guys. That's how she finds out what they're up to.

I want to be just like Dragon-Ella, except I want to be a secret agent instead of a superhero with superhuman strength and laser gaze. I want to fight crime, stamp out evil, and help others, like she does. But my secret weapons are my boots and my Spanish. So I needed practice dealing with bad guys *now*.

But at that moment, I didn't feel like a superhero. All I felt was super unhappy. First, I was stuck working with Johnny Wiley. And now it looked like Abuelita might *really* be leaving us.

I slid my feet onto the couch and hugged my knees. The big old lump in my throat felt like it was going to choke me. I pushed my face against my knees to hide my tears.

Someone sat next to me and slid an arm around my shoulders. I smelled *lavanda* — lavender flowers. That's what Abuelita always smells like.

"*¿Qué te pasa, Gabrielita?*" Abuelita asked me what was wrong.

I shrugged a shoulder.

"*Dime, mi amor.*" Abuelita hugged me. "Tell Abuelita what's bothering you."

I shrugged again. "So many yucky things are happening all at once."

"*¿Cosas malas?*" Abuelita pulled me close. "What kind of yucky things?"

"Well . . ." I wiped my nose and cheeks with my sleeve and looked up at her. "I know you're going back to Puerto Rico. And I don't want you to go. Neither does Miguelito. We need you *here.*"

I looked down at my boots again. Mami walked in from the kitchen.

"Gabí," Mami said, sitting on my other side, "we know you'll miss Abuelita, but you've known all along this was just a visit."

I nodded. "I know, but Abuelita stayed so long this time. And we've gotten so used to having her here. . . . Miguelito and I just hoped . . ."

I glanced up at Mami. She was looking at Abuelita. Her eyes looked like Miguelito's do when he's trying to talk her into something. And her face looked as sad as I felt.

*"Harrumph!"* Papi cleared his throat and knelt in front of me. "Gabita, *recuerda*. If Abuelita . . . goes back home, it won't be forever. She will be back to visit us next year. But your cousins in Puerto Rico miss Abuelita, too. And her house is there."

I just stared back at my boots. I didn't say anything else.

Abuelita kissed my cheek.

"Gabrielita, I'm not going anywhere yet." She gave me a big squeeze. "Why don't we enjoy the time we have together? *¿Qué piensas?*"

"*¡Qué buena idea!*" Mami clapped her hands.

"Tomorrow is Saturday," Papi said. "Let's do something fun!"

"*¡Un día de campo!*" Abuelita took my hand. "We'll go on *bicicletas*!"

I couldn't help grinning. See how *chévere* Abuelita is? How many grandmas want to ride bicycles to a picnic in the park with their families?

That's why Miguelito and I couldn't stand to let her leave us.

"Abuelita," I said, "will you make *pollo frito*?"

"*Con tostones,*" she replied, smiling.

"*Yay!*" Miguelito ran in, bouncing. He must have been listening from the hall. He's always eavesdropping. "*¡Vamos a gozar un montón!*"

"*Sí,*" I said, "we're going to have oodles of fun!"

We both love Abuelita's famous thick-crusted fried chicken and crispy fried green plantains. I couldn't wait to chomp on a fat drumstick!

"And I'll make *escabeche de bacalao*," Mami said.

"*¡Chévere!*" I cried. "Cool!"

That's my favorite salad. It's pickled salted codfish with onions and tiny sour green balls called *alcaparras* — capers. Sounds kind of gross, but it's *yum-yum-yuuuummmy!* I love salty and sour foods.

"*Bien!*" Mami kissed me on the head. "Abuelita and Papi and I will go see what we need for the picnic."

When they left, Miguelito plopped down next to me. "Gabí, I really, really, *really* don't want Abuelita to go! What are we going to do?"

My toes curled inside my cowgirl boots.

My boots usually make me feel like I can do anything. In my boots, I'm Gabí the Great and almost as powerful as Dragon-Ella.

I stomped one red boot. Stomping always makes me feel better.

"Don't worry, Miguelito." I stomped again. "Gabí the Great will figure something out. We won't let her go."

Miguelito squeezed my fingers. "Really?"

I looked down at my little brother. He looked back with trusting eyes.

"I sure hope so."

Maybe tomorrow a super-duper idea would knock me off my boots.

I'd make sure to wear them to our family picnic, just in case.

## CINCO
## CHAPTER 5
## DINOSAUR RAT

"Gabí! Gabí! Gabí!" Miguelito yelled from the edge of a dirt road in the park. "Mami, Papi, Abuelita!"

We had just finished our picnic lunch. The day was really warm and sunny. So we chose a perfect spot that was tucked in the shade of two big oaks. It got kind of breezy and cool in the shade. Abuelita kept pulling her sweater closed.

I was helping Mami clean up and sticking close to Abuelita. (Now that I knew she might *really* be leaving, I didn't want to be far from her.) Papi was putting the leftovers in the basket. Miguelito had wandered off by himself.

"Hurry!" Miguelito called. "¡Avanza! ¡Avanza!¡Avanza!"

"You'd better see what's wrong, Antonio," said Mami to Papi.

"I'll go, Mami," I said. "He probably found some weird bug or worm that he thinks is totally *chévere*."

I hated to leave Abuelita's side, but I needed something to keep me from thinking about her moving away. It gave me the tummy-tingles.

That, and having to work with Johnny Wiley.

*Maybe Mr. F made a mistake,* I kept thinking. *Maybe I'm worrying over nothing. Maybe . . .*

"Gabí!Gabí!Gabí!" Miguelito bounced on his toes the moment he saw me coming. His voice was so loud, my eardrums buzzed.

"Shhh, Miguelito." I covered my ears. "*¿Qué pasa?* What's up?"

He pointed behind him. "*¡Mira!¡Mira! ¡Mira!*"

"Shhhh! Look at what?" Then I saw it.

A few feet away from him, at the edge of the road, lay a big gray mound.

"What is it?" I took Miguelito's hand and tiptoed toward the mound.

"It's a dinosaur rat."

"A WHAT?" I jumped back and pulled him with me. "*¡Caracoles!*"

"A dinosaur rat," Miguelito whispered. "Shhh! I think he's sleeping."

Now *he whispers,* I thought.

"I don't think so, Miguelito," I said. "If he was sleeping, he'd be awake by now."

I stood on my tiptoes and craned my neck. But lots of tall weeds were bent over the mound. So I couldn't see what kind of animal it was.

I curled my upper lip. "Why do you think he's a dinosaur rat?"

" 'Cause he's the biggest rat I've ever seen. He's bigger than Tippy. Fatter, too. And you should see his tail. It's almost bigger than Arturo was."

"EEEIII-OOO!" I shook all over and did a grossed-out, squirmy dance.

Arturo was our pet garter snake. He died last year.

Thinking about a dinosaur rat with a snake-tail gave me the tummy-tingles again. And the tummy-tingles reminded me of Johnny Wiley.

I grabbed Miguelito's hand and ran down the road, dragging him behind me. *Away* from the thing.

"*¡Espera, Gabí!*" Miguelito stopped running and practically yanked my arm off. "Wait, we can't leave. If he's not asleep, maybe he's hurt."

I dug the toe of my boot into the hard dirt road and sighed. "Miguelito . . ."

I like cute little mice and pretty white rats. And Gabí the Great is supposed to help others. But gray rats the size of a fat cat with a tail like a snake, that's asking too much. Even my boots didn't make me feel good about that.

*"Por favor, Gabí."* Miguelito's big eyes started to well up with tears again. *"Pleeeeease!* We have to help him."

"Remember what they told us at the Muir Museum, Miguelito?"

Last summer, Papi took us to the John Muir Wildlife Museum. We went on a tour guided by one of the wildlife experts.

"If you find an injured wild animal," I reminded him, "tell a grown-up. You shouldn't go near it by yourself."

"I know." Miguelito smiled up at me. "That's why I called you."

I grinned. "I know I'm bigger than you, Kikito. But I'm not a grown-up."

I glanced over at the picnic table. Mami was helping Papi bungee-cord the basket to his bicycle. Abuelita was tossing out the last of the trash.

"Abuelita!" I called. "Abuelita, come look at what Miguelito found."

Miguelito bounced. "Abuelita is really good with animals."

"Yup, that's what I was thinking," I said. "She loves them, and they love her."

Abuelita rushed up to us. "*¿Qué pasa, muchachos?*"

"*Mira, Abuelita.*" Miguelito grabbed her hand. "Look at what I found."

I held her other hand, and we led her back toward the dinosaur rat. When we reached the spot where I'd been standing, we stopped.

"*Allí.*" Miguelito pointed to the gray mound. "See over there?"

"We think he's hurt," I said.

Abuelita pushed us behind her. "Stay here, *niños*. Be very, very quiet."

Abuelita picked up a long stick that was lying by the side of the road. She tiptoed up to the still mound. She used the stick to push the weeds aside.

"*¡Ay!*" Abuelita gasped. "*¡Niños, miren!* Look!"

We ran to her side. Now it was my turn to gasp. Miguelito squeaked.

He had been right. The giant rat was bigger than Tippy. Its tail was pink and bald and as long as our snake, Arturo, had been.

And you won't *believe* what was on its back:

Four tiny furry babies with pink noses, feet, and tails!

## SEIS
## CHAPTER 6
## BABIES!

"A mother opossum?" I asked. "Are you sure?"

"*Sí.*" Abuelita nodded, looking down at the scruffy gray thing with the babies on its back. "*Una mamá zarigüeya.*"

"It's not a dinosaur rat?" Miguelito looked pretty disappointed.

"It's something better." Abuelita smiled. "Get your *papi*, Miguelito. Tell him we found an injured mother opossum with babies. Have him empty the picnic basket and bring it here. Hurry up, now. *Avanza.*"

Miguelito tore off to get Papi, yelling at the top of his lungs.

I looked down at the injured mother opossum. Her pointy nose and whiskers reminded me of Johnny Wiley.

*Oops! Here come my tummy-tingles!*

I tried to think of something else. "How do you think she got hurt, Abuelita?"

Abuelita glanced around. "Looks like she got hit by a car or a motorbike when she was trying to cross this dirt road. That happens a lot to wild animals."

I kept looking at the opossums. The babies were wriggling on their mother's back. But the mother hadn't budged since we found her.

"Are you sure she's still alive?" I asked Abuelita.

"*No sé, Gabrielita.* I don't know for sure, but I don't want to touch her until we have to. Wild animals, especially injured ones, get frightened and can bite."

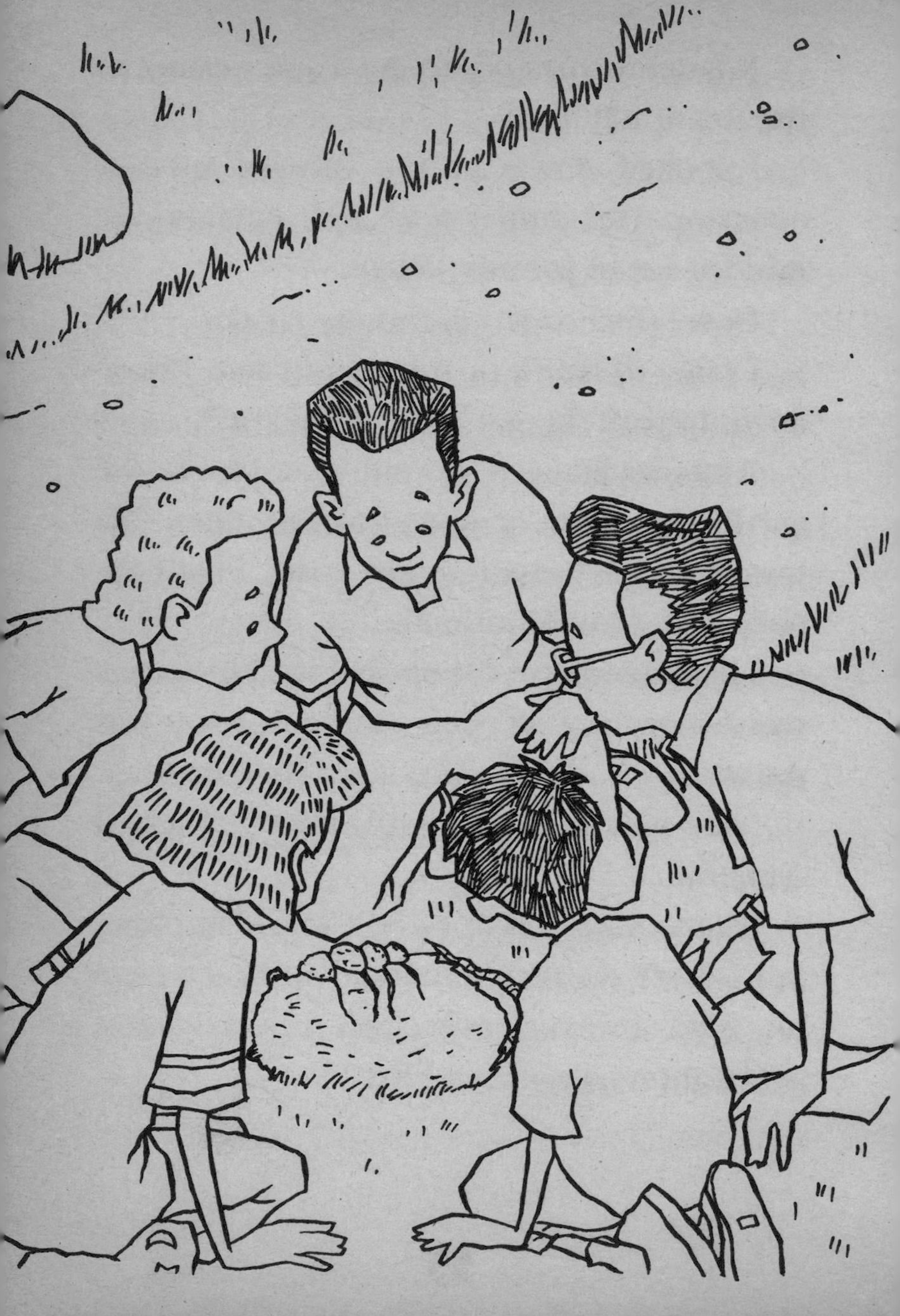

I took a giant step backward — bumping into Papi, who had just run up with the basket. Mami and Miguelito were close behind.

"Stay back with your *mami*, Miguelito," said Papi. "Gabí, you join them."

Papi pulled the big, checkered tablecloth from the basket and folded it a few times. Then he and Abuelita wrapped the mother opossum in it.

He was really gentle when he lifted her into the basket, like when he carries me to bed after I've fallen asleep on the couch watching TV.

I looked up at Mami. "Now what?"

"We'll have to take her to the

wildlife hospital right away," she said. "While they're treating the mother, they can take care of the babies, too."

Miguelito let out a loud wail. "We can't keep them?"

Papi walked up with the basket. "Miguelito," he said, "the mother needs to be in the hospital. And we don't know how to take care of her babies. If they're not cared for correctly, they will die. You want them to be safe, don't you?"

Miguelito nodded, but *se bebía las lágrimas* — he was swallowing his tears. That means he was crying softly.

"Why can't Abuelita take care of them? She's really good with animals."

Mami wiped Miguelito's tears and nose with a tissue. "Remember what they told us at the Muir Museum? People shouldn't keep wild animals as pets. It's not good for the animals."

"But why NOT?" Miguelito whined.

"*Vengan, niños.*" Abuelita took our hands and led us toward the bikes. "We need to hurry and get the opossums some help."

Mami and Papi bungee-corded the basket onto the back of Papi's bike. Abuelita put the leftovers in Mami's knapsack.

While they were busy, I knelt beside Miguelito. He was still sniffling. It made me sad to see him cry.

"Don't worry, Kikito," I whispered. "I'll think of something."

Now I had to figure out how to keep *two* things from leaving us: Abuelita *and* the opossums.

And I still had Johnny Wiley to deal with. *UGH! Here go my tummy-tingles again!*

I looked down at my red cowgirl boots. They were all dusty.

I hope Gabí the Great can work miracles.

## *SEITE*
## CHAPTER 7
## *SAVING THE BABIES*

"You did the right thing by bringing them here," Jackie said. She's the vet's assistant at the John Muir Wildlife Hospital.

"Will the *mami* opossum be okay?" Miguelito asked, sniffling.

"It's too early to tell yet, sweetie." Jackie led us to a sitting area.

"Dr. Sally is still examining her," Jackie told us. "She's a wonderful vet. She'll do the best she can to help the mom. What's important is that you brought them here quickly. That was the opos' best chance of survival."

My forehead crinkled. "Opos?"

Jackie grinned. "It's short for opossums."

"I thought it was a dinosaur rat," Miguelito said, looking hopeful.

"Hey, that's not bad," Jackie replied. "You were pretty close."

I laughed. "He was?"

Jackie nodded. "The opossum is one of the oldest living mammals on earth. It's more than 70 million years old. It practically *is* a dinosaur. In fact, opossums were around when dinosaurs roamed the earth. But it's not a rat. A rat is a rodent, but the opossum is a marsupial."

"A marzipan?" I was totally confused. "I thought marzipan was candy."

"Not marzipan, Gabí." Jackie said the word again, really slowly. "It's mahr-SOO-pee-uhl. A *marsupial* is a type of mammal. The opossum is the only native marsupial in North America. Most marsupials carry their young in a pouch on their bellies."

"Like a kangaroo!" I said.

Miguelito giggled. "We found a dino-roo!"

Everyone laughed. Papi ruffled Miguelito's hair. Abuelita smiled and patted his hand. Mami chuckled and shook her head.

Then I realized something. "But the babies were on the mother opossum's back. Not in a pouch on her belly."

Jackie smiled. "That's because after baby opos are about two and a half months old, they crawl out of their mother's pouch and cling to her back. They stay there until they're old enough to be on their own."

Miguelito's face got all sad again. "So what's going to happen to the baby opos we found? Who will take care of them if their *mami* is too sick?"

"That's a really good question, Miguelito," Jackie said. "We get lots of orphaned wild animal babies here. We nurse them and take care of them until they're old enough to be released back into the wild."

We were all listening really hard. And

Miguelito was nodding, but his eyes were big and sad.

"We also have volunteers who help take care of babies or injured animals in their own homes," Jackie told us.

My eyes practically popped out of my head. Miguelito began to hop. I joined him.

"We can do it!" we both shrieked. "We'll take care of the babies!"

"Whoa! Hold on, you guys!" Jackie held up her hands. "I'm glad you're willing to volunteer, but there's a problem. Under California law, you must be at least eighteen years old to take the wild animals home. And you must complete a training program."

Miguelito's smile faded. He began to whimper. I put my arm around his shoulders and held him close. I felt like crying, too, but I didn't want Jackie to think I was a baby. I really wanted to help save the opos.

Jackie went on. "The good news is that because we're short on volunteers, we're starting a new training program this very weekend. So maybe, if your parents . . ."

Jackie turned to Mami and Papi.

Papi shook his head sadly. "I'm afraid that my wife and I work all day. We simply could not —"

"But Abuelita could!" I burst out. "She can take the training program, and we can bring the babies home!"

"*Yay!*" Miguelito began to hop. "Abuelita is really good with animals!"

"She really is!" I told Jackie. "And she's the right age."

Now we could save the babies!

But I had another reason for wanting Abuelita to take care of the opos. If Abuelita had to take care of them, she would have to stay with us longer. Then maybe she'd never leave.

Phase Two of my Keeping Abuelita Plan: nursing the baby opos.

"Hold on." Mami stood up. "Don't you think we should *ask* your *abuelita* if she wants to do this? Nursing five baby opossums is a very big responsibility."

I turned to Abuelita. All this time, she had been sitting quietly, smiling gently. She had no idea what we were talking about because she didn't speak English.

*¡Caracoles!* Doggone it! That's when I realized my plan wouldn't work. *I should have taught her English weeks ago.* Now I *really* felt like crying.

I swallowed, pushing down the lump in my throat. "Uh, Jackie . . . my grandma only speaks Spanish. Even if she wanted to, how can she take the training program if she doesn't speak English?"

Jackie's face broke out into a big grin.

"That's easy! My last name is Martinez. My parents were born in Mexico. *¡Hablo español, Gabí!* And I'm the one who will be training your grandmother. By the end of this weekend, your grandmother can take the babies home . . . if she's willing."

I nodded at Jackie and crossed my fingers behind my back. I knew Abuelita loved animals. But did she love them enough to stay to take care of baby opos?

I knelt in front of Abuelita and explained everything. "So, will you do it?"

Abuelita looked up at Jackie, then at Mami and Papi, then at Miguelito. Miguelito had his lips sucked in, like he was holding his breath.

Finally, Abuelita looked back at me.

I gave her my best begging-puppy-dog eyes. She can never resist that.

Abuelita spoke Spanish to Jackie. "How long will they need nursing?"

"We're not sure." Jackie shrugged. "Maybe two months."

"*¡Dos meses!*" Abuelita sighed and glanced at Mami. She pulled her sweater close, like she was cold. "I cannot travel while I am caring for the babies."

Jackie nodded. "The baby opos need constant attention. And only a trained volunteer may care for them."

Abuelita looked back at Miguelito, then at me.

She took a deep breath and nodded. "*Muy bien.* Fine, I will do it."

I stuck out my rear and did a hip-wiggle dance. Miguelito bounced.

*"Yippeee!"* we both yelled. "The opos are coming home!"

And Abuelita was staying with us . . . at least for another two months.

I couldn't wait to tell everyone at school!

## OCHO
## CHAPTER 8
## "DISCOVERING OURSELVES"

Johnny Wiley stared at me. I stared back. Our desks faced each other.

It was Monday morning. Our third-grade class was starting to work on our new project, "Discovering Ourselves." In pairs. In pairs of lifelong *enemigos*.

I'd spent the weekend hoping that Mr. Fine would get a clue. I'd hoped he would realize that he'd really blown it: He had picked up the wrong list.

It was all a mistake. The list he had read us was *really* the list of students who should *never* be paired together.

That would make sense. That was the *only* thing that made sense.

But when I had mentioned it to Jasmine, she just said, "Dream on, Gabí girl. Dream on."

So, instead, here we were. Enemy with enemy. Staring at each other. Actually, it was more like *glaring* at each other.

"You're going to teach me Spanish?" Johnny said it the way he would say "You're going to fly to the moon?"

"Yes, already," I said, annoyed. "That's what I'm going to share about my culture."

Johnny grunted, like he still didn't believe me. *If he only knew,* I thought.

"What are *you* teaching *me*?" I asked.

"Well, I'm half Irish and half German." Johnny shrugged. "So I can either teach you to kiss the Blarney Stone or to yodel."

I snorted. "I'd rather kiss a crocodile than kiss

anything to do with *you*. Let's stick to yodeling."

Johnny gave me his Wiley-est smile.

"Hey," I said. "What is yodeling, anyway? It better not have anything to do with
boy cooties."

I wrinkled my nose and curled up my lip
when I said *cooties*.

"Don't worry." Johnny curled up his lip
at me, too. "In order to give *you* boy cooties,
I'd have to touch you and get *Ga-BEE*

cooties. And that's even *worse* than plain old *girl* cooties."

"Good!" I narrowed my eyes at him. "Just so you keep your cooties to yourself. Now, teach me yodeling."

For a second, Johnny got a strange look. Maybe he was thinking. Either that, or he was in pain. Maybe both.

He doesn't do a lot of thinking, so he's not very good at it.

Then Johnny took a deep breath, opened

his mouth, and let out a loud, warble-y yell. It sounded like Tarzan gone wacko!

*¡Caracoles!* I fell right off my seat and landed on the floor. That bad boy *me dio el susto de la vaca,* as Mami would say. He gave me the cow's fright!

*"Hey, that's enough!"* In two steps, Mr. Fine flew across the room.

He towered over us. His bushy eyebrows practically jumped off his face.

"John Wiley, what makes you think that yelling like a banshee is appropriate? And Maritza, what on *earth* are you doing on the floor?" Mr. F pointed at my chair. "In your seat, Maritza. *Now.*"

*Uh-oh!* Mr. F hasn't called me "Maritza" for months — since I changed my name to "Gabí." I hopped up and slid back in my seat.

"John?" Mr. F turned back to Johnny.

Johnny gulped. "I . . . uh . . . was sharing my culture with Mar — I mean — Gabí."

Mr. F's eyebrows squished together to form one long bushy one. *Not* a good sign. I slid low in my seat.

"And what culture would that be, John? A wild banshee culture?"

"No, sir. It's yodeling, sir. From my German side of the family. A banshee would come from my Irish side."

Mr. F's upper lip wiggled. He does that when he's trying not to smile. He swallowed.

"That's quite enough, John," Mr. F said. "You may continue sharing your cultures with each other. But quietly. Like *civilized* people. One more outburst, and you'll both get detention."

Mr. Fine walked up and down the aisles again.

I glared at Johnny. The moment Mr. F was far enough away, I stomped my sneaker. "What's wrong with you? Are you *trying* to land us in detention?"

Johnny blinked. "I was just trying to share my culture with —"

"Oh, yeah? If one of your wacko stunts lands us in detention, I'll share something with you!" I stomped my sneaker again.

My spunky feet would teach him a real *good* lesson!

I wished I was wearing my boots. But Mr. F won't let me wear them to school anymore. The last time I wore them to school was when I almost kicked Johnny. He deserved it. He was teasing my friends and me.

"Oo-ooo, I'm sooo scared!" Johnny made his arms and hands all shaky, like he was really scared.

I sat up on my knees and leaned in toward him. My nose was almost touching his. "You'd *better* be scared!"

"Maritza!" Mr. Fine was standing right behind me. "Sit down. Now!"

I sat. My cheeks burned. It felt like the time I'd put too much *salsa picante* — hot sauce — on my food by mistake.

"I warned you," Mr. F said. "One more outburst, and you'd get detention. Did you think I was kidding?"

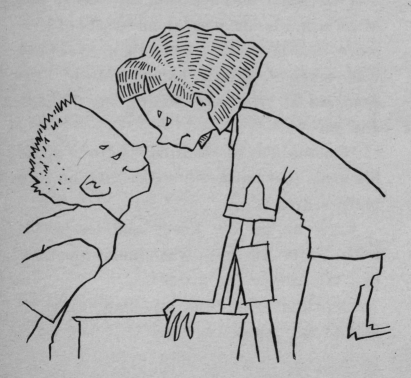

I looked down and shook my head.

"Good. Because I wasn't. You two will spend the rest of this period working together. *Quietly*. I'll see you *both* after school."

Mr. F walked away again.

My toes curled in my sneakers. *I'll fix that Wiley, I'll fix that Wiley, I'll fix that Wiley good!* I thought.

Then I remembered: Mami and Papi seemed really upset last week when I brought home Mr. F's note. But then we all got to go on a family picnic with Abuelita. That's where we found the baby opossums, and that's why Abuelita was definitely staying for two more months.

*Hmmm . . . wait a minute . . . That's it!*

Phase Three of my Keeping Abuelita Plan: Get into *TROUBLE*!

I glanced at Johnny.

*No será cachipa de coco*, as Mami would say. Getting into trouble wouldn't be as easy as pulling the dry shell off a coconut. That means, it was going to be tough. But I had to do it. So I took a deep breath.

"Okay," I said. "It's my turn. I'm going to teach you a Spanish phrase. And you're going to repeat it after me."

Johnny got that look of pain again. *He must be concentrating,* I thought. He's not exactly *un estofón* — the class whiz kid.

I cleared my throat. *"Pareces un perro. ¿Puedo besar tus labios de perro?"*

I repeated the phrase, slowly.

And Johnny repeated each word. Perfectly.

"So, what does it mean?" Johnny asked.

I tried to keep a straight face. "It means, 'Welcome to our classroom. Would you like to sit down?'"

Johnny got that pained look. "Oh, that's a good phrase to know. Teach me again so I can memorize it."

I smiled really big. That was *exactly* what I wanted him to do. That's because what it really means is:

*You look like a dog. May I kiss your dog lips?*

## NUEVE
## CHAPTER 9
# CASTIGOS AND BEST BUDDIES

After school that day, Miguelito and I knelt in the hall, outside Abuelita's room. The door was wide open. We were being super quiet as we watched everything she did.

Only Abuelita is allowed near the baby opos. Those are the rules.

She was feeding them their special opossum formula from a tiny dropper. The wildlife hospital gave Abuelita the formula. It's almost like their mother's milk. Jackie said anything else will kill them.

While we watched, Miguelito was doing the same thing Abuelita was doing. He held a little beanbag squirrel and put a tiny drop-per to its mouth.

He was practicing. Miguelito decided that when he's old enough, he's going to volunteer at the wildlife hospital. He wants to be a vet someday.

When Abuelita was done, she put the babies in a special flannel pouch. Then she placed the pouch in a cardboard pet carrier that the hospital had given her.

She set the box on her desk and gave it a gentle pat. She patted it the way she always pats my hand. But she never said a word.

She's not allowed to talk to the opos. Neither are we. That's so they won't get used to human voices or to being around humans. And we're not allowed to treat them as pets, or name them, or anything. That way, when the hospital releases them, they'll still be wild.

Jackie told us that nature makes wild animals afraid of humans for their own protection. If they were used to being around

humans, they might walk up to a person someday. And that person might hurt them.

*Just as well*, I thought. *If we get too attached to the babies, it'll be harder to let them go. It's going to be hard enough to lose Abuelita.*

Just then, Abuelita stepped into the hall and gently closed the door.

"Gabrielita, I was beginning to worry." Abuelita kissed the top of my head. "Why are you home so late?"

I looked down at my boots. I'd slipped them on the moment I got home. I needed them to help me feel better after detention with Wiley the Smiley.

"I . . . uh . . . I got *un castigo*. Johnny and I got into trouble again. We had to stay after school with Mr. Fine."

Miguelito gasped real big. He covered his mouth with his hand.

"Mami and Papi are going to be so mad!" Miguelito turned to Abuelita. "Will Gabí get a spanking?"

"I do not think so, *mi'jo*." Abuelita sighed. "They do not believe in spankings."

Abuelita turned to me. "But they do believe in *castigos*. They may punish you by not letting you watch television. Gabrielita, why do you do these things?"

"*Lo siento, Abuelita*." I shook my head. "But it wasn't my fault. It was all Johnny's fault. He did this wacko yell and made me fall off my chair. Then Mr. Fine thought we were fighting, and . . . well . . . but I promise, it wasn't my fault."

Abuelita hugged me. "Why don't we go watch a little television now? We can spend some time together. It may be the last television you get to watch for a very long time."

I hugged her back. "Abuelita? Please, please, *please* don't leave us. We need you. *I* need you."

Miguelito joined us for a group hug. "*Sí, Abuelita. ¡No te vayas!* Me and Gabí and you are best buddies."

Abuelita gave a deep sigh and held us close.

She didn't say anything. Maybe she thought that if she didn't speak to us, we'd start getting used to being without her. Like the baby opos.

But it was too late.

The opos might not miss Abuelita when she leaves, but we would.

## DIEZ
## CHAPTER 10
## SISTERS

"Gabí! Gabí!" A voice called from behind us.

Devin, Jazz, and I were walking across the playground before class the next morning. We turned.

It was Cecilia Sánchez. "Little Ceci," we call her. She's my Little Buddy.

In our school, each third grader gets to be Big Buddy to a kindergartner. We get to help them with special projects in class.

Little Ceci moved to California from Nicaragua over the summer. When she started school here, she only spoke Spanish.

Now she speaks English almost as well as Miguelito.

Ceci ran up to us. "Gabí, guess what."

I grinned. She reminded me so much of Miguelito. "What?"

"*Mi tía y mi prima* are here." Ceci was out of breath from running. "All the way from Nicaragua."

"Your aunt and your cousin?" I asked. "Are they staying at your house?"

Ceci nodded. "*Sí*, they will stay with us. But today, Tía Ana and Flor *están aquí, en la escuela.*"

"Why are they here in school?" Devin asked. "Are they moving here? Is your cousin Flor going to go to our school?"

"What grade is she in?" Jasmine asked.

Ceci shook her head. "No, no. They only visit. But Tía Ana is *la directora* of Flor's school — she is like the principal. Flor is old like you, *tercer grado.*"

"Oh." I smiled. "Flor is in third grade, too."

"Do they speak English?" Jazz wanted to know.

Ceci nodded. "Tía Ana speaks very good English. Flor only a little."

"Where are they?" Devin glanced around. "Maybe we can meet them."

Ceci pointed at the principal's office. "She is with Mrs. Ortega."

Jasmine crossed her eyes. "They just arrived and they're in trouble *already*?"

Devin jabbed Jasmine in the ribs with her elbow. "Why are they with Mrs. Ortega, Ceci?"

"That is what I want to tell you." Ceci began to hop on her toes like Miguelito. "They are talking about our schools — Flor's school and ours. *Quieren hacerlas hermanas.*"

Jasmine groaned. "*Now* she slips into Spanish. Right at the good part."

"Chill, Jazz." I turned back to Ceci.

"What do you mean they want to make them sisters? Make who sisters?"

"*¡Las escuelas!*" Ceci hopped on one foot. Her long brown ponytail bounced off her shoulders.

"*What? What!*" Jazz was losing it. "Why does she say all the good stuff in Spanish?"

"The schools!" Devin and I yelled at once.

"The schools?" Jasmine's eyes began to cross on their own. "That doesn't make sense."

"*¿Cómo?*" Now it was Ceci's turn to be confused. "What does she mean?"

"*No tiene sentido,*" I explained to Ceci. "It doesn't make sense. How can schools be sisters?"

"*Sí*, it makes sense." Ceci switched feet, but kept hopping. "They choose *salones* — classrooms. The students write *cartas* and e-mail to each other. The *maestros* even make a web site for the schools."

"¡*Chévere!*" Devin, Jazz, and I yelled.

"It's like being pen pals!" Devin said.

"Do you know which classrooms they're going to choose?" I asked.

Ceci nodded so hard, one of the ribbons flew off her ponytail. The ribbon bopped Jasmine on the nose. Jazz pretended to get dizzy. She stumbled.

Ceci pointed at us. "Yours! Mr. Fine's class!"

Then she thumped her chest. "And mine — the Big and Little Buddies! We will be *hermanas* with Flor's class."

## CHAPTER 11
# CULTURE-SHARING

"All right, Wiley, listen up," I said to Johnny the minute we got paired up again. "We have to get serious about this culture-sharing project. I'm going to teach you some more words in Spanish. And you're going to learn them."

"Then I'll teach you to yodel." Johnny grinned.

I grunted. "We'd better wait till recess for that. I'm not taking another of Mr. F's notes home to my parents because of *you*."

Johnny made a pain-face. I guess he was thinking again.

"Hey!" he said. "You already taught me some Spanish. Why do I have to learn more?"

"Uh . . . because . . ." I tried to think quick.

Last night, I'd realized that Johnny was like a hot firecracker, ready to go off. If he repeated what I taught him . . . well . . . I wasn't sure I wanted to get into THAT much trouble. But how could I stop him?

"Because," I said finally, "it doesn't make sense to tell our class 'Welcome to our classroom. Would you like to sit down?' They're already here, and they're already sitting. But don't worry. I'll teach you some words you'll like even more."

Johnny scrunched up his face. "Oh, I guess . . ."

"Sure," I added, "and you can use the welcome phrase when somebody new comes to class."

*That hardly ever happens,* I thought. *And if it does, Johnny's the one saying it. Not me.*

He shrugged.

"Okay." I nodded. *"Buenos días* means 'good morning.' Can you say that?"

Johnny repeated it. Old Wiley may not be *un estofón*, but he was pretty good at languages.

"Good," I said. "Now, I'm going to teach you *un dicho* — a saying — from Argentina. That's where my *papi* is from. Listen. *Cuando las vacas vuelen."*

I said it once more. Slowly. Johnny repeated it. Perfectly.

"So what does it mean?" he asked.

"It means 'when cows fly.'" I had to giggle. "It's what you say when you don't think something will happen. Or when you don't want to do something."

"Cool!" Johnny nodded. *"Muy* cool!"

"Oh," I said, "you mean, *chévere.* That's how Puerto Ricans say 'cool.' But you got the *'muy'* part right."

Johnny nodded again. *"Muy chévere."*

Just then, Mr. Fine stepped to the front of the room.

"All right, class," Mr. F began. "Last week, I promised you a surprise. Here it is: Mrs. Ortega has been talking with Señora Sánchez, the director of a private school in Nicaragua. They are working on a special program together."

Mr. F's eyebrows wiggled. "We're fortunate that Señora Sánchez and her daughter Flor are visiting our school. Señora Sánchez is Little Ceci's aunt. She and Mrs. Ortega started a program to make the schools be 'sister schools.' I'm pleased to announce that our class will be participating in the program."

Sissy Huffer held up her hand. "What's a sister school, Mr. Fine?"

"Mrs. Ortega, Señora Sánchez, and Flor will explain it to all of you."

Mr. Fine glanced at his watch. "In fact, they should be here any minute. Who would like to be our ambassador? You will open the door, greet them, and make them feel welcome."

Then you won't *believe* what happened next!

Johnny Wiley's hand shot up. He bounced in his chair. "Me! Me! Oh, Mr.

Fine, I know how to welcome them in Spanish. *Pleeeeease,* let *meeee*!"

*¡Caracoles!* My heart just about jumped out of my throat.

"Uh . . . no, Mr. Fine." I barely remembered to raise my hand. "Johnny really doesn't know the phrases that well yet. Could I do it? I'd make a really good ambassador. I speak Spanish perfectly."

"Well . . ." Mr. Fine took off his glasses and rubbed his eyes. He looked kind of tired. "I'm glad you're both so interested in being ambassadors. You seem to be working better together. Maybe the fair thing would be for you *both* to be ambassadors."

Mr. Fine put his glasses back on. "Gabí, why don't you stand by the door and open it when they knock? And since Johnny has just learned some Spanish, it would be nice to have him practice it. Johnny, you welcome them."

I gulped. This was *not* the kind of trouble I meant to get in. And I *never* meant to embarrass Little Ceci or her aunt and cousin. Only Johnny.

I glanced at Devin, then at Jasmine. They had no idea what was going on. I never told them what I'd taught Johnny. I was afraid Devin would give me a major guilt trip.

Before I could think of anything else to do, we heard a loud knock.

"All right, ambassadors." Mr. Fine pointed to the door. "Take your posts."

I jumped up. As Johnny and I walked to the back of the room, I whispered, "Keep it short, Wiley. Just say, *'Buenos días.'*"

"When cows fly!" Johnny whispered back. "This is my chance to show everybody I can speak some Spanish. You just want to hog all the attention."

"I mean it, Wiley! You'll be sorry —"

Another loud knock interrupted what I was going to say.

I glared at Wiley, took a deep breath, and opened the door.

Mrs. Ortega and Señora Sánchez stepped inside. Then Flor and Ceci.

Mrs. Ortega was short and round. Señora Sánchez was even rounder, but much taller.

Flor was taller than me, and skinny. She had the longest, shiniest black hair I had ever seen. It was even longer than Lizzie's. Her skin was the color of very milky cocoa.

*"Bienvenidas,"* I said. I hoped that if I welcomed them first, Johnny wouldn't get a chance to say anything.

Fat chance. Johnny stepped in front of me.

*"Buenos días."* He was so polite, I thought he'd morphed into a nice guy.

He smiled really big at Flor. Flor giggled and looked down at her pretty pink shoes.

I began to relax. But too soon.

Johnny turned to Señora Sánchez and bent forward in a low bow.

*"Pareces un perro."* Johnny's voice was

very friendly. He sounded like he was welcoming them to our school. But he really said, "You look like a dog."

One after the other, each visitor's jaw dropped open.

Then Johnny swished his arm toward four empty chairs. He held out his hand to Señora Sánchez. He thought he was going to ask her to sit down.

I bit my lip. *Parecía que se me iba a ir el mundo*, as Mami would say. I felt like the world was going to fall away and I would faint.

"*¿Puedo besar tus labios de perro?*" Johnny stepped forward. ("May I kiss your dog lips?")

Mrs. Ortega gasped. Her hands flew up to cover her heart.

Señora Sánchez took a step back and shrieked. "*Ooiii!*"

Flor and Ceci sputtered like they were going to spit up their breakfasts.

"What happened?" Johnny squeaked.

Little Ceci stepped up to him. The look on her face said "It's payback time" for all the mean things he had done to her.

"You are *un muchacho muy malo* — a *very* bad boy." Ceci took another step forward. "Do you really want to kiss my aunt's lips?"

Johnny's eyes bugged out. "*¡Cuando las vacas vuelen!* She has girl cooties!"

## DOCE
## CHAPTER 12
# IN THE PRINCIPAL'S OFFICE

*"Es un placer conocerla, Señora Mercado."* Mrs. Ortega shook Abuelita's hand. She told Abuelita it was a pleasure to meet her.

Mrs. Ortega, our principal, was born in El Salvador and still speaks Spanish.

After Johnny did his thing, Mrs. Ortega had yanked us both out of class. Then she called our parents.

She couldn't reach Mami or Papi. So Abuelita came in their place. She stepped into Mrs. Ortega's office.

Mrs. Ortega nodded toward an empty chair. "Please, sit down, Señora Mercado. It is a shame that we first meet on this, uh . . . unhappy occasion."

I sank down in my chair. I wanted to keep slipping down, down, down, until I slid right off the chair. Then I would hide under Mrs. Ortega's desk.

Abuelita sat in the chair next to me. I stared at my sneakers. I couldn't bear to look at Abuelita.

"Gabí is a lively and, uh" — Mrs. Ortega glanced at me — "*spirited* child with a strong will and a mind of her own. Our teachers admire that in her."

Abuelita nodded and patted my hand. I sank lower in my chair.

"But in the last week or so," Mrs. Ortega continued in Spanish, "Mr. Fine has noticed that she's been, well . . . unusually difficult to handle. We were wondering if . . ."

Mrs. Ortega paused and looked at Abuelita. Then she looked at me.

"I am so sorry, Señora Mercado! I haven't

offered you any coffee yet. Gabí, would you ask Ms. Wells to bring in some coffee?"

"*Sí, gracias, Señora Ortega,*" said Abuelita. "I would enjoy some coffee."

I jumped up and stepped out the door. Before the door shut, I heard Mrs. Ortega say to Abuelita:

"We thought maybe Gabí is under some kind of stress. Is something unusual happening at home? Is something troubling her? Perhaps she is acting out to get her parents' attention. Or . . . someone else's . . ."

*¡Ay! Tummy-tingles again!* They hadn't bugged me since the weekend.

I took my time walking over to Ms. Wells's desk. Ms. Wells is the school secretary. I knew there was no hurry to get Abuelita her coffee. Abuelita doesn't drink coffee in the afternoon. She says it keeps her awake at night.

They just wanted to get rid of me. So they could talk.

*¡Caracoles!*

### TRECE
### CHAPTER 13
# PUERTO RICO!

That night before dinner, Abuelita came downstairs after she finished giving the baby opos their six o'clock feeding.

Mami and Papi and I were waiting for her in the family room. Abuelita had already told them about her talk with Mrs. Ortega. Now they would tell me what my *castigo* would be.

"Maritza Gabriela," Mami began, "we are very disappointed in you."

I already knew because she called me by my full name. She only calls me that when she's very unhappy with me.

"I cannot believe that" — Mami stopped for a moment — "that you could play such a mean joke on another student."

Mami swallowed. She glanced at Papi.

Papi looked away. He got real busy searching his pants pocket. He had turned away from me, so I couldn't see his face. But his shoulders were shaking.

Mami took a deep breath and began again. "And what an embarrassment for poor Señora Sánchez! I cannot imagine what she must think of us."

At that very moment, Papi had a coughing fit. He ran to the kitchen.

Abuelita sputtered. She ran after Papi. She seemed to have caught the same cough.

Mami scrunched her eyes shut. Then she

covered her face with her hands. She began to shake.

"*¡Ay, no!*" I cried. "Mami, please don't cry. Please! From now on, I'll be good. Better than good. I'll . . . I'll be an angel!"

At that, Mami sputtered louder than Abuelita had. She collapsed on the couch, roaring with laughter.

In the kitchen, Papi and Abuelita giggled like Devin, Jazz, and I do when we've heard a joke.

Miguelito came running from his room, carrying Tippy. "What's so funny? What's so funny? What's so funny?"

That just made the adults laugh harder.

Their laughter was more catching than a winter flu.

I laughed and I laughed and I laughed. *Reí y reí y reí.*

And Miguelito laughed with us.

Even Tippy laughed. The black spot on his chin wiggled.

After everyone had calmed down, we all sat around in the family room.

Abuelita stood up. "All right, everyone, I have three announcements."

Miguelito gasped. I held my breath. Tippy stopped purring.

"First," Abuelita began,

"I truly believe that Gabrielita will never do anything this foolish again. I know she was very embarrassed and sorry for the humiliation she caused Johnny and the Sánchez family. Isn't that right, Gabrielita?"

I nodded so hard, my teeth rattled.

"Second," she continued, "I do not understand how this family has managed for so many years without me."

"I don't, either," I said.

"Nor I," Papi said.

"Me, neither!" cried Miguelito.

Everyone turned to Mami.

Her shoulders drooped. She sighed. *"Yo tampoco, Mamá. Yo tampoco."*

Papi stood up and took Abuelita's hands. "Please stay with us, Doña Ela. We need you. Every single one of us."

Abuelita smiled. "My third announcement is that I have decided to stay."

*"Yaaay!"* All four of us screamed and grabbed Abuelita in a group hug.

"Wait, I'm not finished!" Abuelita cried after we were done squishing her. "I still need to return to Puerto Rico to take care of my affairs. But I'll wait until the baby *zarigüeyas* are old enough to fend for themselves. And we can all go together. *Como una familia.*"

Mami jumped up and shrieked. "*¡Qué bella idea!* What a lovely idea!"

Mami and Papi linked elbows and did a do-si-do.

Miguelito and I stuck out our rears and did a happy hip-wiggle dance.

"We're going to Puerto Rico!" Miguelito yelled.

"Puerto Rico, here I come!" I shouted. "*¡Aquí viene Gabí!*"

# ¡HABLA ESPAÑOL!
## (That means: *Speak Spanish!*)

**abuelita** (ah-vooweh-LEE-tah): grandma

**abuelito** (ah-vooweh-LEE-toh): grandpa

**abrazote** (ah-vrah-SOH-teh): big hug

**alcaparras** (ahl-kah-PAH-rras): capers

**allí** (ah-YEE): over there

**¡Avanza!** (ah-VAHN-sah): Hurry!

**bebía** (beh-BEE-ah): drank

**bella** (BEH-yah): lovely

**besar** (beh-SAHR): to kiss

**bicicleta(s)** (bee-see-KLEH-tah(s)): bicycle(s)

**¡Bienvenidas!** (beeyem-beh-NEE-dahs): Welcome, ladies!

**cachipa de coco** (kah-CHEE-pah deh KOH-koh) the dry shell of a coconut

**calladito(s)** (kah-yah-DEE-toh(s)): quiet

**carta(s)** (KAHR-tah(s)): letter(s)

**castigo** (kahs-TEE-goh): punishment

**chévere** (CHEH-veh-reh): cool!

**conmigo** (kohn-MEE-goh): with me

**conocerla** (coh-noh-SEHR-lah): to meet you

**cosa(s)** (KOH-sah(s)): thing(s)

**cuchichea** (koo-chee-CEH-ah): whisper

**cuco** (KOO-koh): the bogeyman

**día de campo** (DEE-ah deh KAHM-poh): picnic

**dicho/un dicho** (DEE-choh/oon DEE-choh): a
saying

**directora** (dee-rehk-TOH-rah): director; principal

**¿Dónde está?** (DOHN-deh ehs-TAH): Where is
she/he?

**enemigo(s)** (eh-neh-MEE-goh(s)): enemy/ene-
mies

**escuela(s)** (ehs-KWEH-lah(s)): school(s)

**español** (ehs-pah-NYOHL): Spanish

**¡Espera!** (ehs-PEH-rah): Wait!

**estofón** (ehs-toh-FOHN): a very good student

**familia** (fah-MEE-leeyah): family

**galleta** (gah-YEH-tah): cookie

**gallina(s)** (gah-YEE-nah(s)): hen(s); chicken(s)

**gracias** (GRAH-seeyahs): thank you

**hermana(s)** (ehr-MAH-nah(s)): sister(s)

**hola** (OH-lah): hello

**labio(s)** (LAH-veeyoh(s)): lip(s)

**lágrima(s)** (LAH-gree-mah(s)): tear(s)

**lápiz** (LAH-peehs): pencil

**lavanda** (lah-VAHN-dah): lavender

**lloraba** (yoh-RAH-vah): S/he was crying.

**maestra** (mah-EHS-trah): woman teacher

**malo** (MAH-loh): bad

**meses** (MEH-sehs): months

**mi amor** (mee ah-MOHR): my love

**mi'jo** (MEE-hoh): my dear boy

**mundo** (MOON-doh): world

**muy** (moowee): very

**muy bien** (moowee beeyen): very good; fine

**niños** (NEE-nyohs): children

**¡No te vayas!** (noh teh BAH-yahs): Don't go!

**otra vez** (OH-trah behs): one more time

**pareces** (pah-REH-sehs): you look like

**perro** (PEH-rroh): dog

**pesadilla** (peh-sah-DEE-yah): nightmare

**piso** (PEE-soh): floor

**placer** (plah-SEHR): pleasure

**pluma** (PLOO-mah): pen

**pollito** (poh-YEE-toh): chicken

**pollo frito** (POH-yoh FREE-toh): fried chicken

**presumida** (preh-soo-MEE-dah): stuck-up

**prima** (PREE-mah): cousin

**promételo** (proh-MEH-teh-loh): promise

**puedo** (POOWEH-doh): I can; may I

**puerta** (POOWEHR-tah): door

**quédate quieto** (KEH-dah-teh KEEYEH-toh):
  don't move

**¿Qué piensas?** (KEH PEEYEHN-sahs): What do
  you think?

**¿Qué te pasa?** (KEH teh PAH-sah): What's
  wrong with you?

**reí** (reh-EE): I laughed.

**repite** (reh-PEE-teh): repeat

**susto** (SOOHS-toh): fright

**tercer grado** (tehr-SEHR GRAH-doh): third
  grade

**toma** (TOH-mah): here; take this

**vaca(s)** (BAH-kah(s)): cow(s)

**vamos** (BAH-mohs): let's go

**vengan** (BEHN-gahn): come

**ventana** (behn-TAH-nah): window

**vuelen** (BOOWEH-lehn): fly (as in "they fly")

**yo tampoco** (yoh TAHM-poh-koh): me, neither

**zarigüeya** (sah-ree-GOOWEH-yah): opossum

### #5 All in the Familia

Leaving on a jet plane! Gabí and her family are going on vacation — to Puerto Rico. Gabí and her brother, Miguelito, are super excited (it's their first visit since they were old enough to remember). But Puerto Rico is nothing like Gabí expected. It's hot, even though it's winter. All of Gabí's cousins speak Spanish, but Gabí still can't understand what they're saying. Then Mami and her brother, Tío Julio, get into a contest to see which one will get caught in *un asalto*. But Gabí and Miguelito have no idea what they're talking about or who's going to get caught up in what. Gabí thought visiting Puerto Rico would be fun . . . but it's turning into *un gran* nightmare!